Emmy
the Exaggerating Elephant

Fenton
the Fearful Frog

Gertie
the Grungy Goat

Herbie
the Happy Hamster

Ivy
the Impatient Iguana

Ollie
the Obedient Ostrich

Perry
the Polite Porcupine

Queenie
the Quiet Quail

Rupert
the Resourceful Rhinoceros

Wendy
the Wise Woodchuck

Xavier
the X-ploring Xenops

Yori
the Yucky Yak

Ziggy
the Zippy Zebra

# NOTE TO PARENTS

## Rupert to the Rescue
### A story about resourcefulness

In this story, Rupert the Resourceful Rhinoceros leads a camping expedition which meets with a series of mishaps and near-disasters. Others in the party are discouraged and afraid, but Rupert can always be relied on to come up with an imaginative and resourceful solution to every problem.

In addition to enjoying this story with your child, you can use it to teach a gentle lesson about not giving up when problems arise, and thinking of original ways to help yourself and others.

You can also use this story to introduce the letter **R**. As you read about Rupert the Resourceful Rhinoceros, ask your child to listen for all the words that start with **R** and point to the objects that begin with **R**. When you've finished reading the story, your child will enjoy doing the activity at the end of the book.

The AlphaPets™ characters were conceived and created by Ruth Lerner Perle.
Characters interpreted and designed by Deborah Colvin Borgo.
Cover/book design and production by Norton & Company.
Logo design by Deborah Colvin Borgo and Nancy S. Norton.
Printed and Manufactured in the United States of America

# Rupert to the Rescue

RUTH LERNER PERLE

Illustrated by Richard Max Kolding

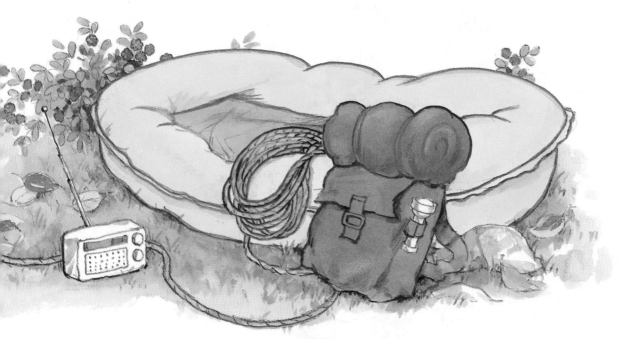

Grolier Enterprises Inc.,      Danbury, Connecticut

One crisp autumn day, Rupert the Resourceful
Rhinoceros said, "This would be the perfect weekend
to go camping on Rugged Ridge Mountain. We'll get a
wonderful view of the changing leaves on the way up,
and on the way back we can raft down Roaring Rapids
River. Who wants to go?"

"I'll go!" said Yori the Yucky Yak. "Maybe I'll see some
snakes and spiders!"

"I guess I'll go," said Una the Unhappy Unicorn. "It
will give me something to do."

"Count on us!" said Delilah the Demanding Duck and
Xavier the X-ploring Xenops.

"I'll go too—*if* I don't forget!" said Albert the Absent-
minded Alligator.

"You'd better know the way, Rupert!" said Delilah. "I don't want to get lost."

Rupert unfolded a map and pointed to a steep mountain road. "See?" he said. "First, we'll hike along Rolling Rock Trail to the top of the mountain. Then we'll cross the bridge over Rumble Ride Ravine to go to the old abandoned gold mines. We'll camp at the bend of the river, and the next morning, we'll row our raft downstream, back to the bottom of the mountain."

"That seems like a long and hard trip!" Una said.

"It is," agreed Rupert. "But it will be lots of fun."

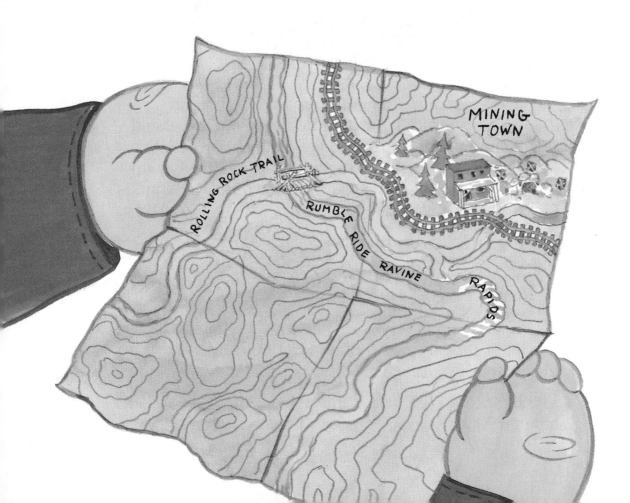

That afternoon, the AlphaPets gathered all the things they would need for the trip.

Delilah, Yori, and Una arranged backpacks, sleeping bags, and blankets.

Albert loaded his wagon full of cans of rice soup and ravioli, packages of hot dogs and rolls, boxes of raisins, and bags of marshmallows.

Rupert folded his rubber raft and tied it with a strong rope. He put a flashlight, trash bags, and a first aid kit in his pack.

Xavier brought his radio, some matches, a pocket knife, and a compass.

Early the next morning, everybody was dressed and prepared for the camping trip.

"Is everybody ready?" called Rupert.

"You bet!" Xavier shouted. "Lead the way!"

"Don't forget the food, Albert!" said Delilah.

Just as they were about to leave, some of the other AlphaPets came to wish their friends a safe trip.

"We'll wait for you by the river when you return tomorrow evening," they called.

The hikers waved and started their climb up the mountain trail.

"I hope they don't trip and fall!" whispered Fenton the Fearful Frog.

"I hope they have enough of everything," shouted Emmy the Exaggerating Elephant.

"I hope they have a wonderful time," whooped Herbie the Happy Hamster.

After the campers climbed for a while, they stopped to rest. Xavier turned on his radio. They listened to some music while they had something to drink.

Suddenly, the AlphaPets heard a terrible rumbling above them. Rupert looked up. A giant jagged rock was rolling down the side of the mountain!

"Look out!" cried Xavier. "It's a landslide!"

Everybody jumped out of the way as the rock crashed down and stopped in the middle of the road.

"Oh, no!" cried Una. "Now we're stuck. There's no way we can get past that rock."

"Maybe we'd better go back," suggested Albert.

"No way!" Rupert cried. "Not as long as we have all this good rope with us."

"What's the rope got to do with it?" asked Delilah.

"You'll see," said Rupert, taking the rope off his raft.

The AlphaPets watched Rupert tie knots all along the length of the rope. Then he made a big loop at one end.

"If I can get this rope to hook onto the top of that rock, we'll have a perfect ladder," he said.

Rupert tossed the rope up as far as he could, but it did not catch on the rock.

"Forget it!" said Una. "We're doomed."

Rupert tried again and missed.

He tossed the rope up one more time. This time it hooked onto the top of the rock and held tight!

"Now, we can use the knots as steps and climb up. Then we'll slide down the other side," Rupert said.

Carefully, Rupert climbed to the top of the rock and tied the rope securely. One by one, he helped his friends climb up and then slide down on the other side.

When they were all safely over the rock, Delilah pointed at Albert and said, "Oh, no! You forgot the food!"

"What will we eat? We'll all starve," cried Una.

"We'll think of something," Rupert said. "Let's get going. We need to be at the bridge before dark."

Before long, the AlphaPets came to Rumble Ride Ravine. The mountain seemed to split in two and there was a deep canyon below.

"We can cross over there," Xavier said, pointing to a narrow bridge. "I'll go first."

But when Yori followed . . . *CRACK!!*

The bridge started to split right down the middle!

"Help!" screamed Yori. "Save me!"

"Hold on, Yori!" Rupert called. "We can fix the bridge."

Rupert showed Delilah and Albert how to use vines to tie together the small logs they found. Then Rupert slid them over to Yori.

"Tie the logs to the rails," cried Rupert, "while we go get some more vines. Be careful!"

Everyone helped, and finally, they were able to cross the bridge safely.

"Phew! Now all we have to do is get to the old mine and set up camp," Rupert said.

Everything was quiet at the old mine. The AlphaPets
looked around at the rickety buildings and the
abandoned railroad tracks. There were mine shafts and
caves everywhere.

"Look at all those caves!" Xavier shouted. "Let's see
what's inside them."

Everyone followed Yori into the entrance of the cave. It was dingy and damp, and streams of rusty water trickled down the walls. *Drip. Drip. Drip.*

"This place looks haunted!" Una cried.

Then Albert felt the ground move under him. WORMS!! "*Eeek!*" he screamed.

"What's the matter, Albert?" Yori said. "These worms won't hurt you. See how cute and squiggly they are?"

"Yech! Let's get out of here!" Delilah yelled.

The AlphaPets ran down to the river.

"Now, where did you say we're going?" Albert asked.

"Never mind *where*. The question is *what*. What are we going to eat? We're all hungry, and there's no food," said Delilah.

"No problem!" Rupert said. "I have an idea. Una, bring me two long sticks. Albert, please unravel the red tassel on your hat while I find some paper clips in my pocket. And Xavier, you can use your matches to start a fire."

"How will that feed us?" Delilah demanded.

"You'll see!" answered Rupert.

Using the sticks and other materials, Rupert made two good fishing rods.

"You're a genius!" said Xavier.

Then Yori and Delilah sat by the edge of the water and caught enough fish for everyone.

While Albert grilled the fish on the fire, Una and Rupert picked red raspberries for dessert.

It was a delicious meal, and everyone felt better after they ate. As the sun was setting, the AlphaPets admired the brightly colored autumn leaves.

"So far so good!" Rupert said. "We'll sleep here, and tomorrow we row down the river."

The AlphaPets climbed into their sleeping bags and fell fast asleep.

In the morning, everyone helped Rupert inflate the big rubber raft. They huffed and puffed until the raft was nice and plump.

"We need to rig up a ramp to launch our raft," Xavier said. So Rupert brought an old door from the mine and everybody pushed the raft down into the water.

While they were pushing, *rrripp!* The edge of the raft caught on a nail. *Phhhh!* All the air leaked out.

"Oh, no! Now we'll drown for sure," Una sobbed.

"Don't give up!" said Rupert. "There's plenty of old wood and nails at the mine. We can build a raft. Then it will be smooth going to the bottom of the mountain."

Everybody helped, and when the raft was finished, they carried it to the water and pushed off.

Soon everyone was feeling much better as they drifted down the river.

Suddenly, they heard water rushing in the distance.

"That must be the rapids!" Rupert said. "They sound rough. Maybe we should go ashore and carry our raft."

But it was too late! At the bend, the river turned into a roaring waterfall.

"Hold tight everybody!" Rupert shouted. "We're going for a ride!"

The rapids pushed the AlphaPets over the side and smashed most of the raft to bits!

Rupert looked around. Una, Delilah, Albert, Yori, and Xavier were all clinging onto pieces of the broken raft and swimming toward shore.

"We made it!" Rupert shouted.

Suddenly the frightened AlphaPets heard a rustling behind the bushes. They could hear footsteps crackling on the fallen leaves.

"Who could that be?" Delilah shouted.

The footsteps came closer and closer.

"Who's there?" cried Xavier.

"It's us!" called a familiar voice. "We're here to welcome you back home."

There, coming through the bushes, were Herbie, Emmy, and Fenton.

Rupert jumped up. "It sure is good to see you again!" he cried.

Everybody gathered around.

Yori put his arm around Rupert and said, "We're tired and dirty and ragged and rumpled, but thanks to you, Rupert, we're all all right!"

Here are some useful words to know.

rope

raisins

raft

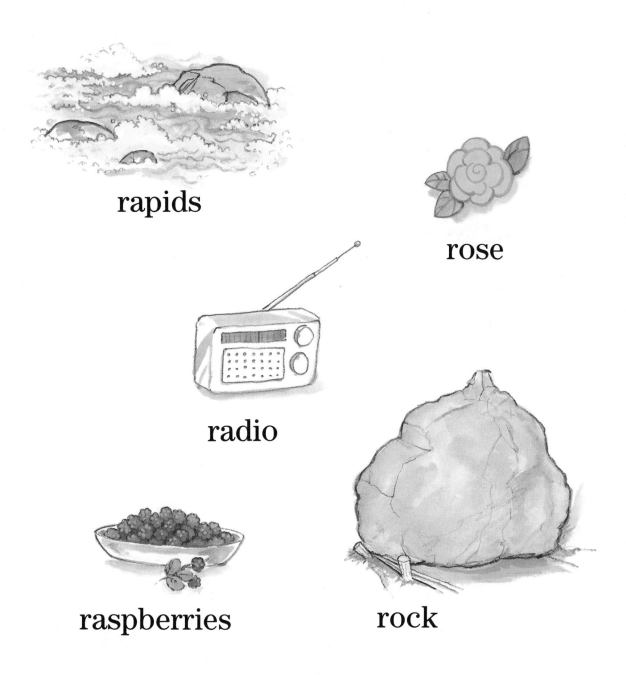

rapids

rose

radio

raspberries

rock

Look back at the pages in this book and find these and other words that begin with R.

# Aa Bb

# Gg Hh

# Mm Nn Oo Pp

# Uu Vv Ww